A FREE TRANSLATION
FROM THE FRENCH
OF CHARLES PERRAULT

CINDERELLA

or The Little Glass Slipper

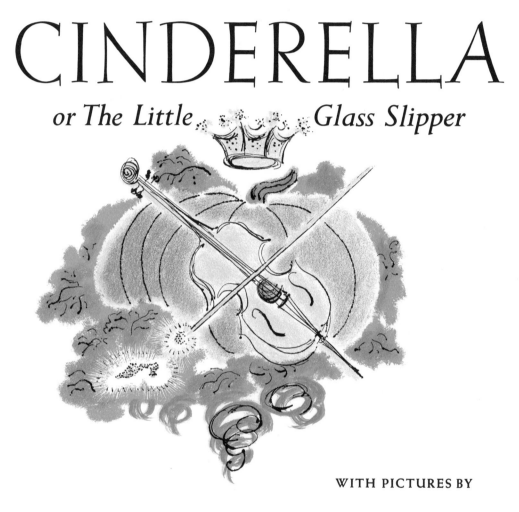

WITH PICTURES BY

MARCIA BROWN

Troll Associates

FOR MARY GOULD DAVIS
WHO UNDERSTANDS
THE TRUE SPIRIT
OF
CHARLES PERRAULT

Printed in the United States of America
10 9 8 7 6 5

CINDERELLA

Once upon a time there was a gentleman who took for his second wife the proudest and haughtiest woman that was ever seen. She had two daughters who were just like her in every way, bad disposition and all. The husband had a young daughter of his own, but she was sweet and good. She took after her mother, who had been the best in the world.

The marriage ceremony was hardly over when the stepmother's temper flared up. She could not abide this young girl, whose goodness made her own daughters seem more hateful than ever. She gave her the vilest household tasks; it was Cinderella who scoured the pots and scrubbed the stairs, Cinderella who polished the bedchamber of madame and also those of her daughters.

Cinderella slept on a wretched straw pallet in a miserable garret away up in the top of the house. Her sisters lay on beds of the latest fashion in fine chambers with inlaid floors and great mirrors in which they could admire themselves from the tops of their silly heads to the bottoms of their feet.

The poor girl put up with everything. She dared not complain, even to her father. He would only have scolded her, because—alas!—he was tied hand and foot to his wife's apron strings.

When her work was done, Cinderella would creep to the chimney corner and sit there in the ashes, earning for herself the nickname, Cinderseat. But her younger step-sister, who was not quite so rude as the elder, gave her the name of Cinderella, and Cinderella she was. In spite of her rags, however, Cinderella was a hundred times more beautiful than her sisters, for all their fine clothes.

Now it happened that the king's son was to give a ball. He invited everyone who was anyone, including our two young misses, for they cut quite a figure in the land. They were delighted with themselves, busy as you please choosing their costumes and headdresses to go with them. More work for Cinderella, for it was she who starched their linen and puffed their ruffles. Chitter chatter of nothing from morning to night but what they would wear and how they would look.

"I," announced the elder, "shall wear my cherry velvet with the English trim."

"As for me," said the younger, "I have nothing but my usual petticoat, but to make up for that, I shall wear my cloak of flowered gold and my diamond circlet, which is not to be sneezed at either."

They sent for the best hairdresser to pile their curls into two horns. None but the best beauty patches would do. They called in Cinderella to ask her advice, for she had very good taste in these matters. Cinderella gave them the best advice in the world and even offered to dress their hair, which of course was what they really wanted in the first place.

While she was working over them, they would say to her, "Cinderella, now wouldn't you just like to go to the ball?"

"Oh, you are making fun of me. A ball is not for such as I."

"You are right. Cinderseat at a ball! How people would laugh!" And they laughed themselves at the very thought.

Someone else would have made nests of their heads, but not Cinderella. She was good. She dressed them perfectly.

The two sisters were in such a twitter of excitement that for two days they hardly took time to eat. They strained and snapped a dozen corset strings, pulling them too tight in order to shrink their waists. All day long they paraded in front of the looking glass.

At last the happy day arrived. They departed, and Cinderella followed them with her eyes as long as she could. When she could no longer make them out she began to cry. It was all in tears that her godmother found her.

"Why, what is the matter, my child?"

"I wish . . . oh, I wish . . ." Cinderella was so choked with tears that she could not get her words out.

Now Cinderella's godmother was really a fairy. She said to her, "You wish you could go to the ball, is it not so?"

"Oh yes," sighed Cinderella.

"Well, just be a good girl," said her godmother. "I'll see that you go."

She took Cinderella into her chamber and said, "Now, go into the garden and bring me a pumpkin." Cinderella ran to look for the most beautiful pumpkin she could find and carried it back to her godmother. How on earth could a pumpkin take her to the ball? Cinderella could not guess. Her godmother scooped the pumpkin all out, leaving only the rind. Then she touched it with her wand, and— just like that! the pumpkin turned into a beautiful coach, gilded with pure gold.

The fairy godmother then went to look for the mousetrap. In it were six sprightly mice. She told Cinderella to lift the door of the trap, and as each mouse scampered out she tapped him with her wand. Each mouse was instantly turned into a handsome, spirited horse. And there, all in all was a fine set of six horses, of a beautiful, dappled mouse-grey.

Now for a coachman. "I'll go and see," said Cinderella, "if there's a rat in the rat-trap. We can make a coachman out of him."

"You are right," said her godmother. "Go see."

Cinderella brought the rat-trap. In it were three plump rats. The fairy chose the one that had the most handsome whiskers. When she touched him with her wand—there was a sleek coachman with the most elegant mustaches you have ever seen.

Then the fairy godmother said to Cinderella, "Go now into the garden. Behind the watering pot you will find six lizards. Bring them to me."

Cinderella had hardly fetched the lizards when her godmother turned them into six footmen, who hopped up behind the carriage in their fancy livery and lace and held on as if they had never done anything else in their lives.

Then the fairy said to Cinderella, "There now, that will take you to the ball. Are you not pleased?"

"Oh, yes, but must I go in these rags?"

Her fairy godmother had scarcely touched Cinderella with her wand when her rags changed into a gown of gold and silver, embroidered with rubies, pearls and diamonds. Then— she gave her a pair of little glass slippers, the prettiest in the whole world.

Thus arrayed, Cinderella climbed into the coach. But her godmother charged her above all, "Do not stay a moment after midnight. If you do, your coach will turn back into a pumpkin, your horses into mice, your footmen into lizards and your riches into rags."

Cinderella promised her godmother that she would not fail to leave the ball before midnight. Away she went, beside herself with joy.

Now when the king's son learned that a grand princess, whom no one knew at all, had just arrived at the palace, he ran out to receive her. He offered her his hand as she alighted from the coach and led her into the ballroom, where all the company was assembled. Then—a deep silence fell over the room, everyone stopped dancing, the violins stopped playing, all eyes turned to the great beauty of this mysterious one. Only a low murmur rippled over the gathering, "Oh, how beautiful she is!"

The King himself, old as he was, could not take his eyes off her and whispered in a low voice to the Queen that it had been a long time since he had seen anyone so charming and beautiful.

The ladies were busy studying her headdress and her gown in order to have some made just like them the next day. If only they could find stuffs as fine and workmanship as skillful!

The young prince conducted Cinderella to the seat of greatest honor and then led her out on the floor to dance. She danced with so much grace that people wondered at her more than ever.

A most splendid feast was served, but the prince did not taste a mouthful, so intent was he in gazing at Cinderella.

Cinderella went to sit near her step-sisters and paid them a thousand courtesies. She shared with them some oranges and lemons which the young prince had given her. The sisters were completely astonished. They did not recognize her at all.

Suddenly Cinderella heard the clock chime eleven hours and three quarters. She immediately made a deep curtsy to the company and hurried off as quickly as she could.

When Cinderella got home, she went to look for her god-mother and thanked her. Then she told her how she longed to go to the ball the following night. The prince had *begged* her to come.

While she was telling her godmother everything that had happened at the ball, her two step-sisters knocked on the door. Cinderella ran to let them in.

"How late you are!" she said, yawning, rubbing her eyes, and stretching as if she had just waked out of a sound sleep. (While they were gone, she had had no wish to sleep!)

"If you had come to the ball," said one, "you would not have been bored, I can tell you. A most beautiful princess came, the most beautiful princess anyone could hope to see. She paid *us* a thousand courtesies; she gave *us* oranges and lemons."

Cinderella was delighted. What was the name of this princess?

They answered, "No one knows. The King's son is desperate. He would give anything to know who she is."

At this Cinderella smiled and said softly, "She was then so beautiful? My goodness, how lucky you are! Would I could see her! Ah, Mademoiselle Javotte, lend me your yellow outfit that you wear for every day."

"Really," said Javotte, "I like that! Lend my clothes to a filthy Cinderseat like you? I should be mad!"

Cinderella expected this snub. She was secretly relieved, for what would she have done if her sister had been willing to lend her her dress?

The next night the
two sisters were off again to
the ball, and so was Cinderella, but this
time even more splendidly dressed than before. The prince
never left her side. All evening he paid her charming compli-
ments. The young miss found this so far from boring that she
forgot her godmother's warning. She was horrified to hear the
first stroke of midnight before she thought it could be eleven
o'clock. She rose and fled as lightly as a doe. The prince
followed her, but he could not overtake her. In her haste,
Cinderella dropped one of her glass slippers. The prince
gathered it up with the greatest care.

Cinderella reached home all out of breath, with neither coach nor footmen, and in rags. Nothing was left of her finery but one little slipper, the mate to the one she had lost.

The guards at the palace gate were questioned. Had they seen a princess leave? No, they had seen no one but a young woman in rags, and she looked more like a peasant girl than a fine young lady.

When the two sisters returned from the ball Cinderella asked them if they had enjoyed themselves again and if the beautiful lady had been there. They told her, "Oh, yes, she was there, but at the stroke of midnight she fled from the palace. She dropped one of her little glass slippers, the prettiest in the world. The King's son found it, and he did nothing but gaze at it, all during the rest of the ball. He certainly has fallen head over heels in love with the owner of the slipper."

They spoke truly, for a few days after the ball, the King's son had his herald

sound throughout the land
that he would marry her whose
foot would fit the little slipper. First
they tried it on princesses, then on
duchesses and all the ladies of the court,
but it was no use.

They brought it to the two sisters, who did their best to
force their feet into the little slipper, but they could not.

Cinderella was looking on and recognized her slipper. So
she laughingly said, "Let me see if it would fit me." Her step-
sisters burst into shrieks of laughter. Fit her! Oh! Fit Cinderseat!
How they mocked her. But the gentleman who had been sent
to try on the slipper looked intently at Cinderella. Finding her
beautiful, he said it was no more than right. He had been
ordered to try it on all the young ladies.

He had Cinderella sit down, and
sliding the slipper on her little foot,
he saw that it fitted her perfectly, just as if it
had been made of wax. The astonishment of her sisters was
great, but greater still when Cinderella drew from her pocket
the little slipper which she slipped on her other foot.

Then suddenly, her godmother appeared.
Touching Cinderella's rags
with her wand, she changed
them into a costume still
more magnificent than any
she had worn before.

Now her step-sisters
recognized her. Cinderella
was the beautiful personage
they had seen at the ball!
They threw themselves
at her feet and begged
forgiveness for all their
bad treatment of her.
Cinderella asked them
to rise, embraced them
and told them she forgave
them with all her heart.
She begged them to
love her always.

Cinderella was conducted to the young prince, dressed as she was. He found her lovelier than ever, and a few days afterwards, married her. Cinderella, who was as good as she was beautiful, gave her sisters a home at the palace and on the same day married them to two great lords of the court.